W9-AHW-846

The BACKYARDIGANS™

Follow That Egg!

adapted by Catherine Lukas
based on the original teleplay by Adam Peltzman
illustrated by The Artifact Group

Ready-to-Read

SIMON SPOTLIGHT / NICK JR.
COOPERATIVE LIBRARY SERVICES
New York   London   Toronto   Sydney

Based on the TV series *Nick Jr. The Backyardigans*™ as seen on Nick Jr.®

SIMON SPOTLIGHT
An imprint of Simon & Schuster Children's Publishing Division
1230 Avenue of the Americas, New York, New York 10020
Library of Congress Cataloging-in-Publication Data
Lukas, Catherine.
Follow that egg! / adapted by Catherine Lukas ; illustrated by The Artifact Group. —1st ed.
p. cm. — (Ready-to-read)
"Based on the TV series Nick Jr. The Backyardigans as seen on Nick Jr."
ISBN-13: 978-1-4169-5040-0
ISBN-10: 1-4169-5040-0
I. Artifact Group. II. Backyardigans (Television program) III. Title.
PZ7.L97822Fo 2008
2007007529

5201 9550 6/13

"Look! King PABLO has

a job for us," says TYRONE .

"Ready, Knight UNIQUA ?"

"Ready, Sir TYRONE !"

"I know! Maybe King  PABLO

needs us to go up DRAGON MOUNTAIN,"

says Knight UNIQUA.

"We knights do not mind

a big job.

We might even see a ,"
DRAGON

says Sir .
TYRONE

"Brave knights, I must go
to the  store.
I need a new ,"
says King .

"Your job is to take care of this  while I am gone. Please keep the EGG safe and sound."

"An  ?" asks [UNIQUA].
EGG

"An [EGG] does not move

at all," says [TYRONE].

" [DRAGON] [MOUNTAIN] would be more

interesting."

The starts to roll.
EGG

The rolls away.
EGG

"Stop that ! "
EGG

yells Knight .
UNIQUA

The  rolls
EGG

down the 🪜 ,
STEPS

through the 🚪 ,
DOOR

and into the 💧 .
WATER

"Follow that  !"
EGG

yells Sir .
TYRONE

The  floats to the
EGG   FOREST

of the Grabbing Goblin.

"The Grabbing Goblin

will grab the !" says
EGG

Knight .
UNIQUA

"Watch out!"

Someone grabs

their ,
HELMETS

their ,
SHIELDS

and then the !
EGG

"Grabbing Goblin!"

says Knight  .

UNIQUA

"Give back that !"

EGG

It is too late.

They all go over

the  .

WATERFALL

Hooray! They catch the ! EGG

Crack!

Now the  has ! EGG LEGS

The  runs away. EGG

They pass the Fairy .
HOUSE

Fairy  wants the  too!
TASHA   EGG

She tries to take it.

Crack!

Now the has !
EGG   WINGS

The flies away.
EGG

It flies up  .
DRAGON   MOUNTAIN

"The  is in danger!"

EGG

says Fairy .

TASHA

"Oh, no! What if a gets it?"

DRAGON

asks Sir .

TYRONE

"We have to save the !"

EGG

At the top of  DRAGON MOUNTAIN,

Sir TYRONE finds an empty

shell. Did the EGG hatch?

"Ah! A DRAGON !" yells AUSTIN.

"Run!"

They run. Then they fall.

A baby catches them.

DRAGON

"Look what hatched from

the !"

EGG

says Knight .

UNIQUA

"We have to show the king!"

says Sir .

TYRONE

King  returns.

PABLO

He has a new CROWN.

"I see the EGG hatched,"

he says.

"I hope it was no trouble."

"Not for brave knights like us!"

says Sir .

TYRONE

"Good," says King  .

PABLO

"I knew you could do the job.

Come to my 🏰 for a snack!"

PALACE